A FABLE FOR PARENTS

The WORLD of the CHILD

by Aline D. Wolf

Illustrated by
Anna Marie Magagna

Parent Child Press   Altoona, Pa.

P.O. Box 767
Altoona, Pennsylvania 16603

Backward, turn backward, O Time,
in your flight,
Make me a child again
just for tonight!

Elizabeth Akers Allen

"Daddy, Todd is picking up those dirty stones," Ginny tattled as we stood in line to go into *The World Under the Sea* — the biggest attraction in *Wonder World*. I stooped to the level of our two-year-old as he grasped a handful of pebbles mixed with sticky caramel corn.

"Todd, let go of that stuff." Todd tightened his chubby fingers around the glop in his hand and looked up at me. "Todd . . . I said drop it." But Todd didn't let go. I had to pry open his fingers and shake the gooey mess from his hand. "You can't pick up stuff that everyone has walked on. It's loaded with germs. . . . AND PLEASE, KEEP YOUR STICKY HANDS OFF MY TROUSERS."

"Don't yell at him like that," Laura, my wife, snapped. "He's been pretty good considering he's so young to come to a park like this."

"We should have left him home," I told her. "It's going to be one of those days. Look at this line. I can't even see where it starts."

"Daddy, he's doing it again; he's going to eat that dirty popcorn." This time I gave him a little slap and knocked the stuff from his hand. Todd started the funny whine that always led into his loudest cry.

"Why don't you buy him his own box of popcorn?" Laura suggested. "Then he'll forget about what's on the ground."

"He'll only spill it, just like he dumped the whole box of cereal on the kitchen floor this morning. That's what delayed us — cleaning up that mess. And now everyone else is ahead of us in line."

Todd's cry was reaching its peak and people started to stare at us. I picked him up in my arms and his loud cry slowly subsided into quiet sobs.

"I never cried like Todd does. Did I, Mommy?" Ginny asked in her superior tone of voice.

"Sure you did," Laura told her. "You just can't remember."

"I can too. I can remember lots of things." She thought for a moment. "I can remember the old house where we used to live and the day that Todd was born and . . ."

"Yes, but you were six years old then. I'm saying you can't remember what happened when you were one or two."

"What did happen then?" Ginny suddenly wanted to know.

"Well, you learned to talk . . . and to go up and down steps . . . and to feed yourself. Do you remember the first day you ever used a spoon?"

Ginny wrinkled her nose. "No, I guess I can't. . . . Why can't I, Mommy?"

"It's just one of those things that's hard to explain. But don't worry about it; nobody else can remember the first two years either."

"Todd, get your hands off my face," I blurted as he suddenly clapped his sticky palms on my cheeks. I was losing my patience.

"Laura, it's crazy to wait in this line. Let's take them to something else. *Jungle World* looks pretty good."

"No," Ginny pleaded, "please, Daddy. I'm the only one in my class who hasn't seen the real shark in *World Under the Sea*. Please. . . . "

"We did promise Ginny we'd go to this one," Laura reminded me.

"Well if YOU want to wait in this line then YOU take them yourself. I've had it!"

"Okay, okay. I'll take them myself. You go and do something else for a while; maybe you'll feel better later. Where will you meet us?"

"How about *Ice Cream World*?" I felt I owed them a treat.

"All right," she agreed. "But it will be an hour or more. . . . "

"I'll be waiting."

I walked away, thinking I would look for some target shooting. It was a warm Sunday afternoon in October and the park was filled with the color of cotton candy and the smell of roasting hot dogs.

In the distance I could hear periodic screams from people riding the *Roller Coaster*. I passed the candied-apple stand . . . *The Dodgems* . . . and an old man carrying an enormous cluster of brightly colored balloons. As I approached the *Merry-Go-Round*, the calliope was playing the same tune I remembered hearing many years before, when I was a little boy.

The wooden horses on the carousel, bearing children of all ages, hadn't changed over the years. They had the same prancing feet, the same flourishing tails. Old memories came back to me as I watched the carousel going around and around. . . . When I was a child I always wanted to get on a horse that went up and down rather than on one that stood still. . . . I could remember

begging my father many times for "one more ride". . . . and then I remembered a very old feeling of being scared on one of the high horses because my short legs couldn't reach the stirrups.

As I reminisced, the circular motion began to make me feel dizzy. I closed my eyes for a minute and when I opened them again I noticed the balloon man was moving to another location. His massive array of balloons glided past me, and I was suddenly facing a building that I hadn't noticed before. It had a plain blue door and a sign, *The World of the Child*. I wondered what was in there. Maybe they had toy trains like the ones I had when I was a kid. Thinking it would be fun to run those old trains again, I decided to go inside.

When I reached the door I could see sticky fingermarks near the knob. There was graffiti too. *"You have been here before but you cannot remember."* Graffiti writers were all jokers. *"You will be frightened, frustrated and impris . . ."* The last word looked like "imprisoned" but it was too blurry for me to be sure.

The blue door creaked eerily when I opened it. Inside there were no little trains or any other toys — just a long stairway going up. The light was dim and I couldn't see all the way to the top. Nobody else was around. Suddenly the door slammed shut behind me, abruptly quieting the calliope music and dimming the light even further. I began to climb the long stairway.

After going up several steps I tripped. What a strange stairway! Each step was a little higher than the one before it. I had to lift my feet higher and higher for each step. Midway I stopped to rest and I noticed that the step ahead of me, instead of being a few inches above my ankles, was almost up to my knees.

The handrail, too, was now higher than when I started. I had to strain my arm to reach it. Gradually my fingers slipped away from the railing and I just wasn't tall enough to grab it again. Without the help of the handrail I was afraid of falling backwards. Almost without thinking about it, I dropped my hands to the step ahead of me and began going up on my hands and knees. In this position, I could climb easily by putting my knee, rather than my foot, on each new step.

My eyes gradually became accustomed to the dim light. Ahead of me at the top of the stairway, I could see a large panel of wood, which blocked my way completely. I stared at it for a few seconds, wondering how I could get beyond it. Then I looked up and several feet above my head was a large round metal object attached to the right side of the panel. I finally figured out that it was a door knob.

A door knob! I was facing the largest door I had ever seen. Straining on tiptoes, I tried to reach the knob but it was just beyond my fingertips.

I knocked on the door, but instead of a strong rap, my knuckles made only a timid sound. Probably no one inside could hear it.

But someone did. Loud clicking steps approached and the door was opened by a hand somewhere above a pair of long legs in high heels. My eyes were staring straight into the hem of a skirt. She was a giant lady, or maybe even a lady giant! I had to tip my head back to see all the way up to her face.

"Hi there, Punkin," she said in a cooing voice, as if I were a baby. "I was wondering where you were." That was a strange way for her to greet a visitor. She sounded as if I lived in this place. Was it possible I had been here before? "Look how dirty you are!" she said, reaching down with one of her giant hands to brush a cloud of dust from the knees of my trousers. Her movement was so quick and unexpected that I almost lost my balance. I guess she didn't know I had to come up those steps on my knees.

The giant lady turned and walked away from me at a very fast pace. What big feet she had! What long steps she took! When she reached the other side of the room, she sat down on a giant-sized chair and began talking on an enormous telephone.

I stared at everything around me, hardly believing what I was seeing. The walls were four times as high as I was. The window was so far above my head that through it I could see only the sky. Across the room where the giant lady was sitting, there was an unusual collection of legs. The table had six legs that were taller than I was. Each of the four chairs had four legs. The giant lady's legs were angled among the four legs on her chair. Her high heels were hooked on the rung of her chair so that her enormous knees were staring at me. I couldn't see what was on the table, only what was under the table.

I wanted to find out more about this crazy place. . . . I turned toward the wall with the high window and saw a row of doors that were just my size. They didn't have high doorknobs way above my head. They had metal handles which I could easily reach.

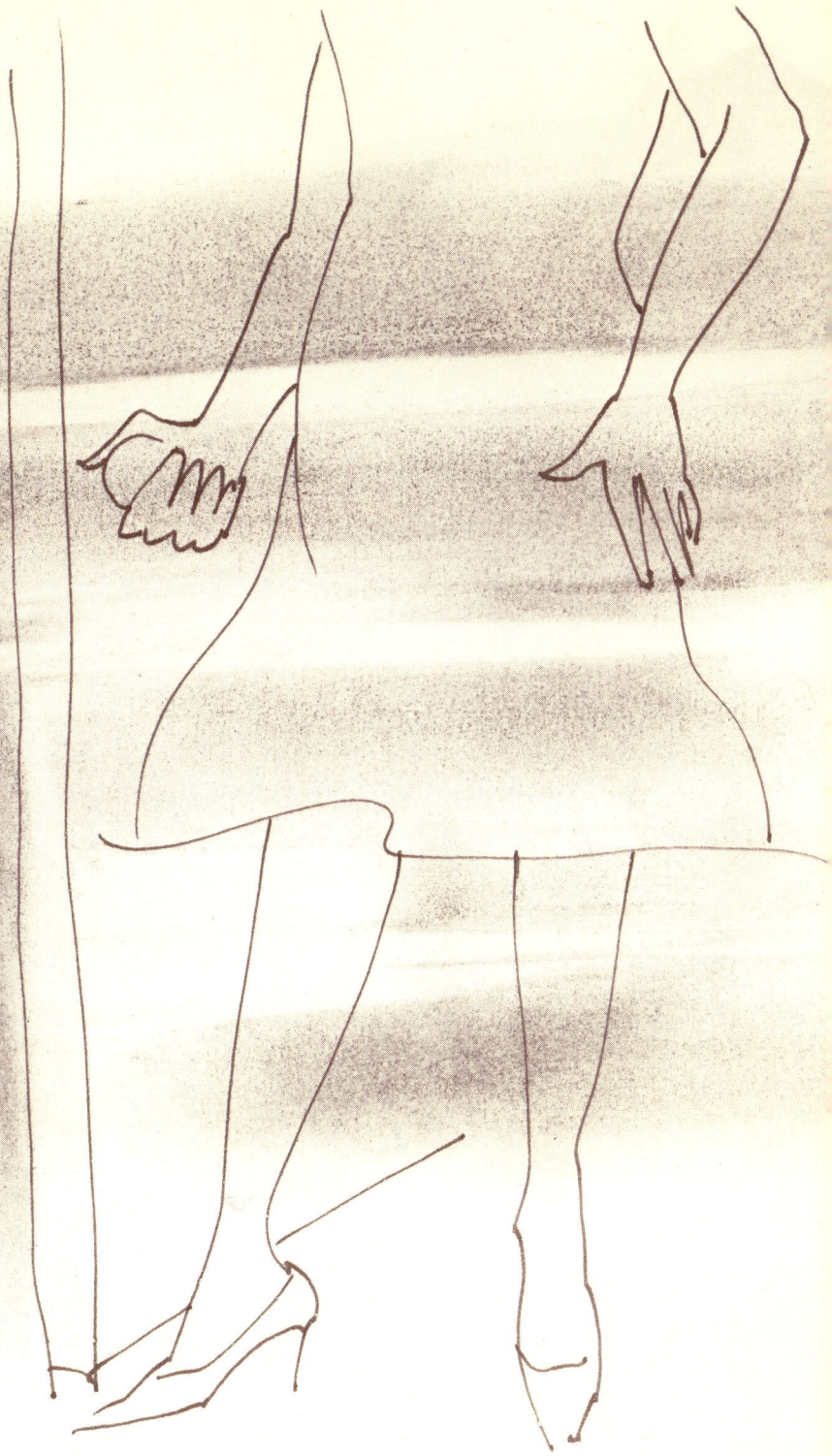

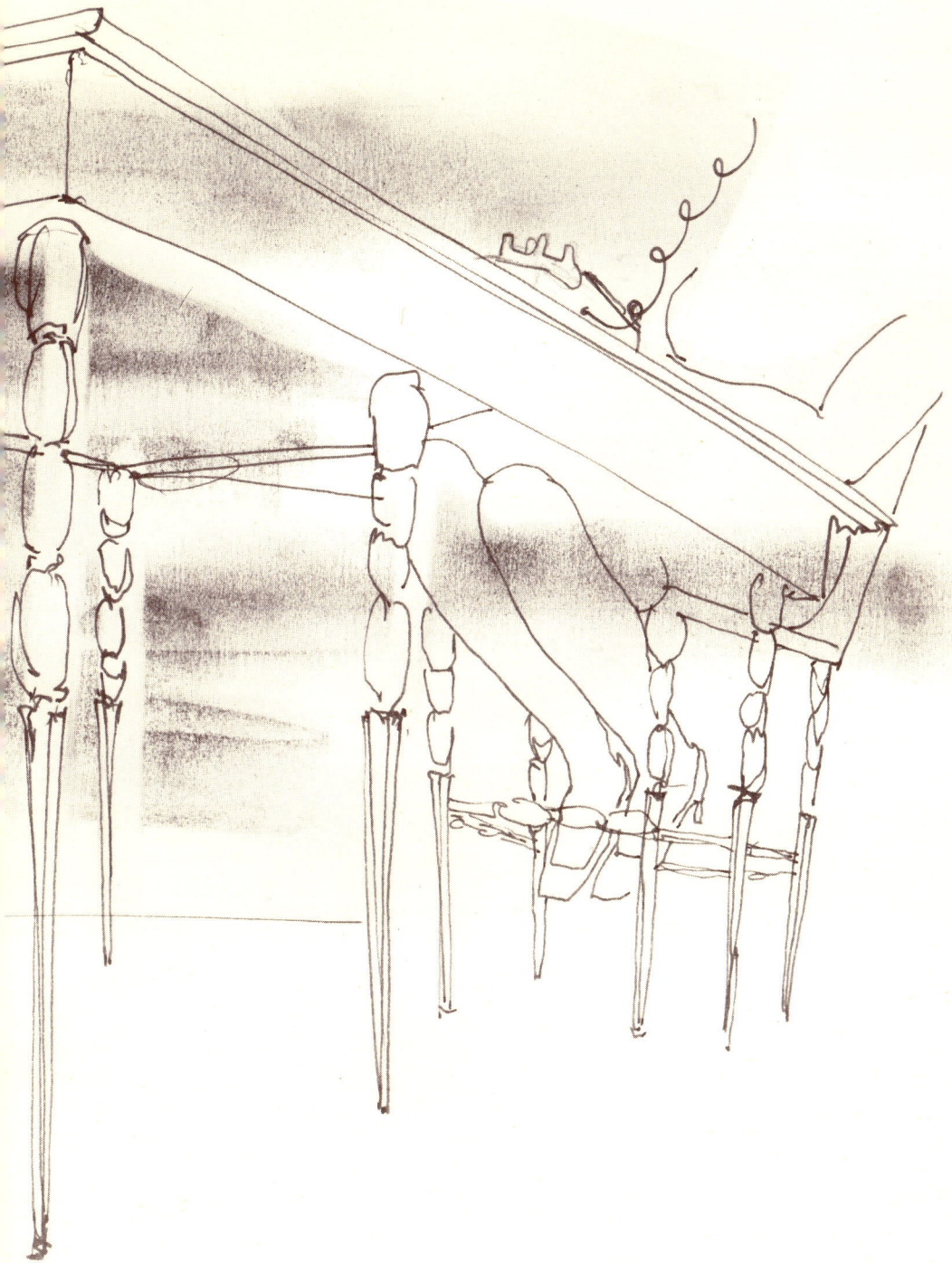

As I started to walk toward the row of doors, I noticed that my sense of balance was changing. My head seemed to be getting heavier and I began walking hesitantly as if I were top-heavy and about to fall at any moment.

I kind of staggered across the room, feeling as if I were going to topple forward. After a few steps I fell but didn't hurt myself. I wanted to stand up again but there was nothing nearby to support me. So I

crawled on the blue and white linoleum toward the row of doors. Where had I seen that blue and white linoleum before? Somewhere . . . Some place . . .

Suddenly an enormous brown furry animal came into the room. He rushed toward me with his mouth open, revealing large pointed teeth and a red tongue that looked two feet long. He barked in my ear and I screamed in terror.

"Honey, don't be afraid of Copper. He won't hurt you. He's only a dog."

I was so scared I could hardly understand what the giant lady was saying. She pulled my hand toward the animal. "Here, Honey, I want you to pet Copper." Obviously she didn't know that the monster would chew my hand off if I put it near him. But I knew! I screamed louder and kicked my feet on the linoleum. "We'll have no temper tantrums," the giant lady announced firmly as she forced me to pet Copper.

Terrified I held my breath. Suddenly everything turned black.

When I opened my eyes again, I was in the giant lady's arms. She was hugging me and kissing my forehead. "Everything is okay now, Honey; I put Copper in the basement. He can't hurt you. Now dry your tears." I tried to control myself but big sobs kept coming back. My mouth and throat felt very dry.

Then a loud bell rang. The giant lady put me down on the floor and answered the phone on the other side of the room. My whole body was sweating. I tugged at the sleeves of my sweater and managed to take it off. Where should I put it? No way could I reach the coat hook that was on the back of the big door. So I left my sweater on the floor and crawled over to the row of doors.

I pulled open the first door and was surprised again. Instead of another room there was a giant-sized closet with two shelves. Wow! What huge pots and pans. I pulled the tallest pot out on the floor beside me. It was almost as high as my waist. Then I pulled out a frying pan so wide I could have sat in it. And what was this other funny thing? I began pulling a handle attached to a wooden cylinder about five inches in diameter. When I pulled it off the shelf, the tremendous weight made it slip from my grasp. It rolled across the floor — a rolling pin longer than a yardstick!

"Oh dear!" the lady giant whined. "Look at this mess. You know you aren't supposed to get into the cupboards."

I started to pick up the frying pan to put it back on the shelf. But she took it out of my hand and clanged all the things back into the cupboard. Then she slammed the door. I decided not to open the other doors right now.

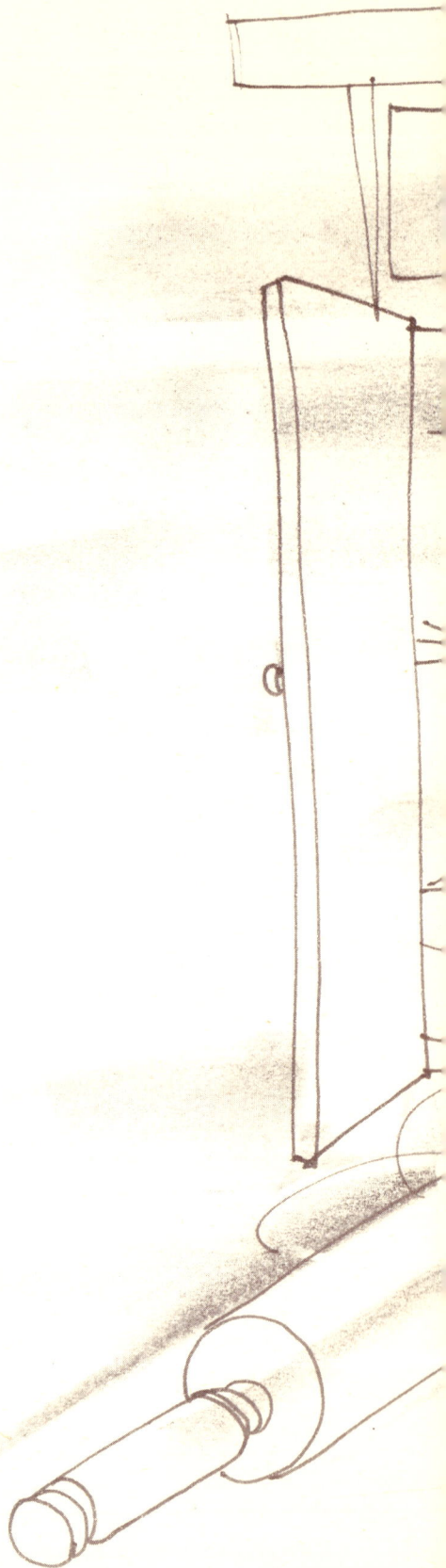

"When will you learn not to throw your sweater on the floor?" she scolded as she picked up my sweater and hung it on the high hook on the door. The hook was even higher than the door knob. I wondered how she had expected me to reach it.

"Look at your hands," the giant lady groaned, "all dirty from crawling around here. You'll have to wash them before lunch."

I looked around wondering where to wash my hands. The only possibility was the big brown basin of water on the floor. There was no soap so I just splashed my hands in the water. Then I heard the giant lady running toward me again.

"Get out of the dog's bowl," she yelled. "You have water all over the floor. What am I going to do with you?" She grabbed a huge paper towel and wiped up the water.

"Come into the bathroom with me," the giant lady ordered as she took my wet hand and dragged me down the hall. I did my best to walk as fast as she was walking but my legs were much too short.

"Now, let's wash your hands," she commanded as we reached the sink. At least I think it was a sink. It was so high that I couldn't peek over the edge of it. She pulled my hands forward as far as they would reach and let some water run over them. "Here's the soap," she said, handing me a bar of soap as big as a loaf of bread. My fingers weren't long enough to hold it firmly and it slithered to the floor. I stood there with my hands dripping water on the linoleum. "Look at that," she said crossly. "That is the umpteenth mess you've made today. I'll have to get the mop." All of a sudden I realized who this giant lady was. She was the custodian here. Her job was to keep everything neat and clean.

"Well, it's time for lunch," the giant lady announced as she finished her mopping. This time instead of pulling me along the hall, she picked me up in her arms and carried me to the kitchen where she put me on one of the big kitchen chairs. The table in front of me was just even with my chin so I decided to kneel on the chair to make myself higher. At last I could see what was on the table — several giant-sized bowls, great big knives and spoons, a jar of peanut butter that was the size of a bucket and a box of cereal that seemed three feet tall.

The giant lady went over to the stove and began stirring something in a large pot. "I'm making some pudding for your lunch," she said. I was pretty hungry so I decided to have a little cereal while I was waiting. I lifted the cereal box and tilted it toward one of the bowls. But the box was so top-heavy that the cereal rushed into the bowl and overflowed onto the table and the floor.

While she was cleaning up the cereal, the pudding began to burn. She rushed back to the stove. "Today is one of those days — just one thing after another. I guess you'll have to have cereal for lunch after all."

She poured some milk on the cereal in my bowl. "Here you are," she said, handing me an enormous serving spoon. "I am going to teach you to feed yourself." She put her huge hand over mine and helped me to spoon the cereal to my mouth. The tip of the giant serving spoon just fit between my lips.

"You're doing fine," she told me. After helping me with several spoonfuls, she went over to the sink to wash the burned pot.

When I tried to eat by myself, I found it awkward to get the large cereal flakes on the spoon, so I just ate them with my fingers. I was still very thirsty

from crying but there was no glass or cup on the table. So when I finished the cereal I drank the milk that was left in the bowl. Because the bowl was much too wide for my mouth, two streams of milk rolled down the front of my shirt. The giant lady came running over to me again and wiped my shirt with a towel. "Thank goodness," she said, "it's time for your nap."

A nap? Why did I have to take a nap? I didn't feel tired at all; I wanted to spend all the time I could exploring this giant house. I tilted my head back, looked at the lady giant and managed to say "No." She didn't pay any attention to my word. She carried me down the hall to another room where there was a bed about six feet above the floor with a high fence around it. Without any warning, she put me on the mattress inside the fence. Then she leaned over and kissed my cheek. "Have a nice nap, Honey," she called, as she closed the great big door.

This was a ridiculous
situation. Here I was —
penned in by a fence that
came up to my chin.
Certainly I could get out of this.
I grabbed the rungs and tried
to put my leg over the top.
But I just wasn't tall enough.
Maybe if I shook the fence,
I could get part of it to fall
down. I shook it as hard as I
could, making a terrible racket,
but the fence wouldn't move.
I wondered how long I
would have to wait for the
giant lady to return and take
me out of my prison.

After what seemed like a very long time, the big door of the bedroom swung open. Another surprise! This time a giant man came in. "Hi there, Buster," his voice boomed, "I'm home early today. Mama went to the supermarket." He swooped me up in his arms and gave me a hug as if I were his child. "You little rascal, I'll bet you didn't sleep a wink." He threw me up in the air. My heart jumped as I whirled toward the ceiling. Then I began to fall swiftly — terrified that I would land with a crash. But his big arms caught me before I touched the floor and he whirled me through the air again. "How's that for a ride?" he asked.

He held me in his arms so I could look straight at his great big face. "Say, 'I'm Daddy's boy,'" he told me. "Let me hear you say, 'I'm Daddy's boy!'" There was something vaguely familiar about his words, but I couldn't remember where I had heard them before.

The giant man carried me out to a room with a great big desk. "You play on the floor here while I finish my paper work," he told me. "I have to put these reports in the mail before five."

He put me down on the floor, wound up a toy monkey and set it down in front of me. The monkey danced around the floor with jerky movements. I wondered what I was supposed to do with it.

I wanted to explore the rest of the giant house so I left the monkey dancing there and sneaked out of the room. In the hallway I came to a giant-sized mirror. When I stood close to it, my breath blew a misty cloud on the glass. The cloud hid my face and I looked like a body without a head. I looked so funny that I started to laugh. Then I blew more breath on the mirror to make more of myself disappear. My shoulders disappeared, then my arms. I laughed louder.

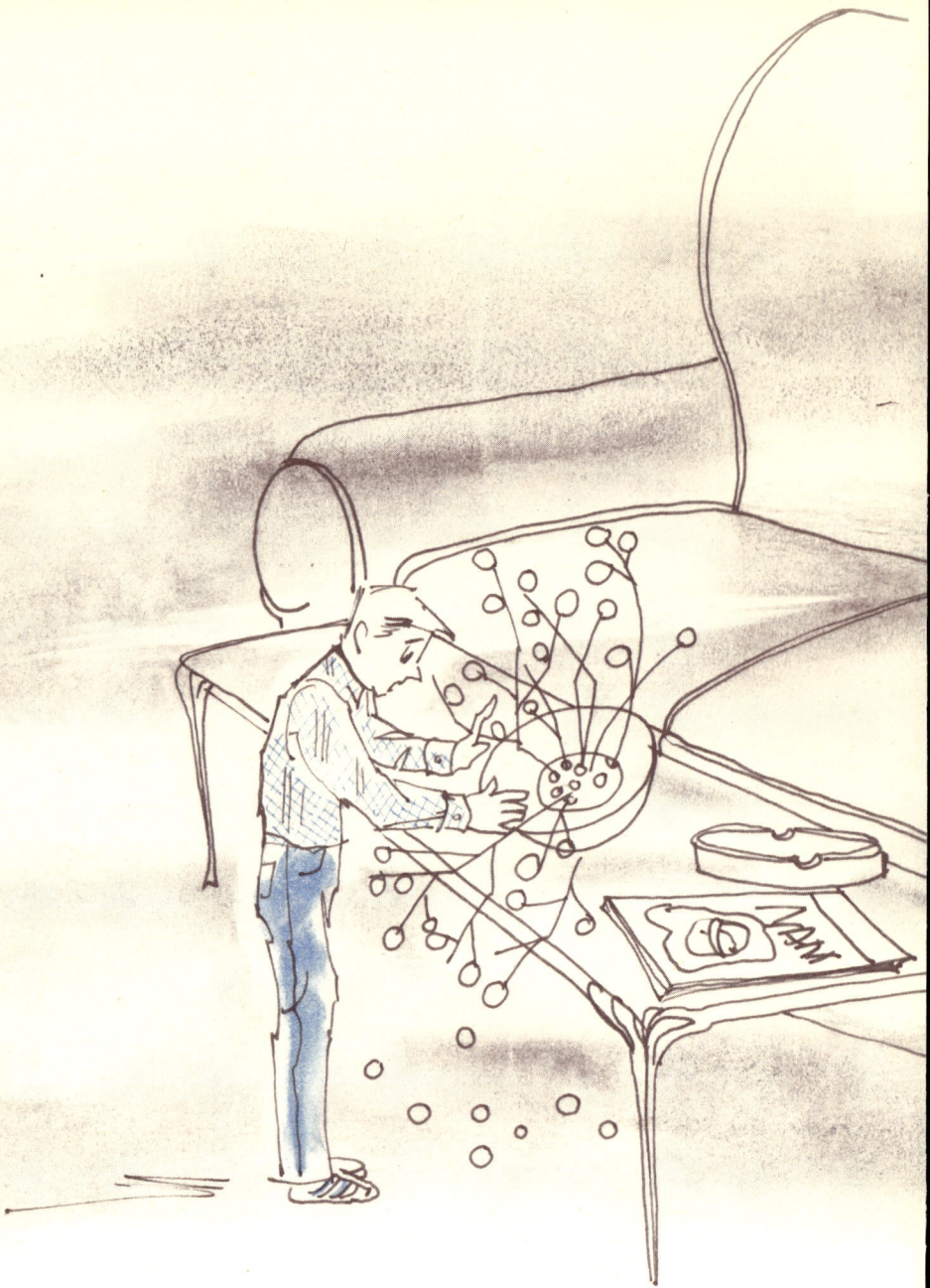

"What's going on here?" the giant man asked as he approached. I pointed to the mirror expecting to hear a giant laugh that would shake the house. But he didn't think it was funny. These giants didn't have any sense of humor.

"You better not put any fingermarks on the glass," he cautioned. He was a custodian, too.

I continued walking down the hall in my slow clumsy way and found a big room with a light blue carpet. There were huge pieces of furniture covered with fine soft material in lovely pastel colors but they were all too high for me to sit on. In front of

the giant-sized sofa was a table that was the right
height for me. I could reach everything on this table. There was an ash tray that looked like a basin.
There were magazines as big as newspapers and
beside them a bowl with a tree growing out of it.
On the branches of the tree were pumpkins. But
what funny pumpkins! They seemed to be made of
velvet. I wanted to feel them to be sure. But as soon
as I touched one of them the whole thing toppled
over and crashed on the table.

"What are you doing?" the giant man called.
"You know you're not allowed to play in the living

room. Wait till Mama sees this. She just made that Halloween decoration yesterday." He led me quickly to the kitchen.

"We're going to walk to the mail box," he said as he took my sweater down from the high hook on the big door.

"I'll put your sweater on you," he said. He put his giant hand around my wrist and shoved one arm into the sleeve, then the other arm into the other sleeve. I started to button the bottom button, but as I was trying patiently to get it in the button-hole, the giant man took over the job. "When are you ever going to learn to do things for yourself?" he asked. Then he buttoned all the buttons himself.

He looked at his watch. "We'll have to hurry; the mail pick-up is at five o'clock."

We went outside and the giant man started to walk quickly down the street. But I had to look at everything around me. Wow! The bushes were as tall as I was and the trees were at least fifty feet high. Under one of the trees there were some inter-esting rocks. Some of them had a brownish cast over their basic grey color. These would be great for my rock collection! I stooped down to take one.

"Drop that," the giant man ordered as he knocked it from my hand. "That's dirty. You can't pick up stuff that everyone has walked on. It's loaded with germs." I wondered where I had heard those words before.

He took my hand and started pulling me with him. I had a very hard time keeping up with him. My head was still so heavy that I tottered when I walked. Finally, I tripped but his strong arm kept me from falling on the sidewalk.

"Well, well, well! What's going on here?" I heard a new voice and turned to see another man who looked like a giant grandfather. He was down on his knees working in a garden so I didn't have to tilt my head back to see his face.

"Hello, Harry," the first giant man said to him. "We're trying to get to the mail box before five."

Harry looked up with a smile. "This fellow is having a hard time trying to keep up with you. Why don't you leave him here with me while you mail your letters?"

"Good idea, Harry. I'll be back in a few minutes." He continued down the street, taking enormous giant steps.

Harry was digging holes in his garden. "Come over here, young fella, and I'll show you how to plant some bulbs." He had a bulb in his hand that was the size of a grapefruit. "Watch!" he said. "I'll put the bulb in this hole and cover it up with dirt. It will stay in the ground all winter. When the weather gets warm in the spring some green stalks will grow out of the bulb and come up through the ground. After a few weeks, there will be a beautiful flower. How about it? Would you like to plant one of these bulbs?" he asked. I smiled at him.

"You're going to need some tools," he said, "but my tools are too big for you." Harry's watering can was as high as my elbow, and I knew my hand wouldn't fit around the handle of his digging tool.

"Over here I have some smaller tools that I bought for my grandson," he said as he walked toward a very large shed.

In a few minutes he returned with a smaller watering can and a digger which just fit my hand. This was fun! I dug a deep hole. I put a shiny brown bulb in the hole and covered it with dirt. Then I held my watering can high and watched the water sprinkle the ground. I wondered if I could remember where I had planted my bulb because I wanted to come back to see the flower in the spring.

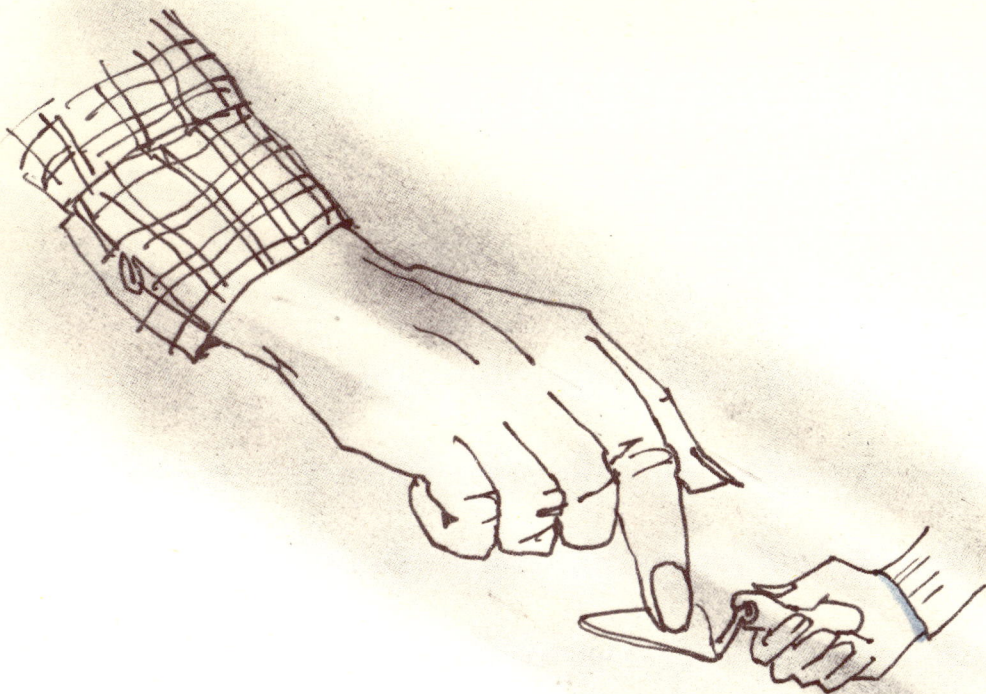

As I stood up, I noticed that the sun was getting lower in the sky. How long had I been in this place with the giants? Maybe two or three hours. I had forgotten about Laura and Ginny and Todd. They must still be waiting for me at the *Ice Cream World*. Suddenly I knew I had to find that long stairway behind the big kitchen door. I had to find it right away.

Harry seemed to understand my concern. "Well, young fella, maybe your visit here has been long enough for you to learn a few things. If you want to go back to *Wonder World* now, I'll walk over to the stairway with you." He took hold of my muddy hand; the dirt didn't bother him at all.

We walked back to the house at a comfortable pace. He took me into the kitchen and opened the big door. There was the long, dimly lighted stairway that I had come up on my knees. I felt terrified when I looked down. I stood there paralyzed — afraid to attempt even the first step.

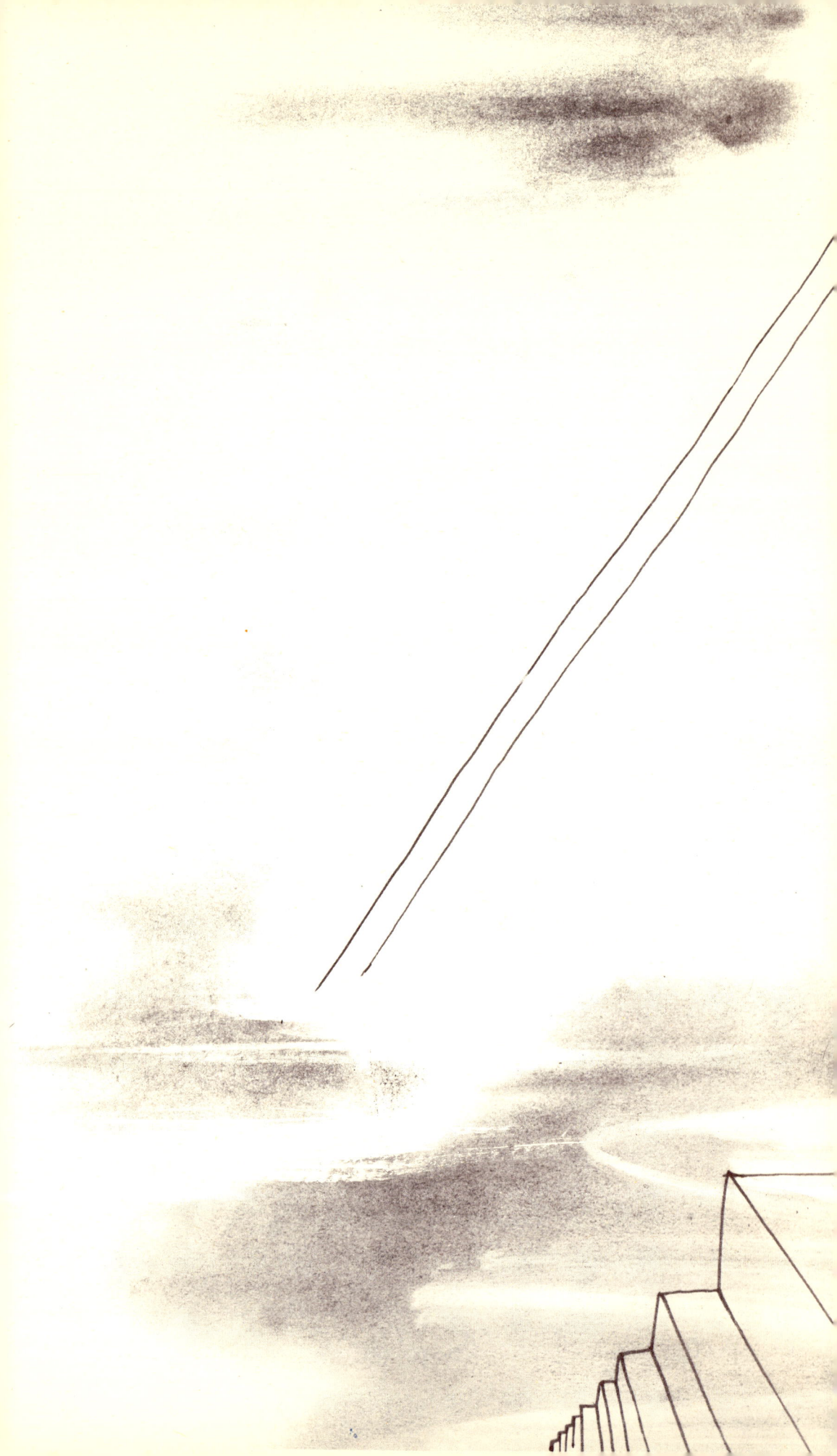

"Just hold my hand," Harry said. "I'll walk down with you at least part of the way."

We started down the very high steps and I managed pretty well with Harry holding my hand. As we descended the steps, each one seemed a little shorter than the one before. When we were almost at the bottom, they became normal-sized, at least normal for me. Harry's giant-sized feet hardly fit on the step.

"This is about as far as I can go," Harry said. "You reach up there and grab the handrail. You won't have any trouble from here." As I ran down the last four steps, I could hear the calliope music faintly in the distance. The blue door swung open and the music suddenly became louder. I turned to wave good-bye to Harry, but I could no longer see him on the dimly lighted stairway.

My knees were shaking from the effort of walking down those terrible steps. As I emerged from the semi-darkness, the late afternoon sunlight was a shock to my eyes. It seemed weird to see everything in normal size again. People of ordinary height were all around me, walking at their usual pace. I was looking at their faces instead of their knees. The carousel was still going around, the calliope was playing the same tune and the balloon man was back where I had first seen him.

"Daddy!" Ginny's voice startled me as she ran toward me. "Where were you? We waited at the *Ice Cream World* for a long time. Then Mama said we should look over here for you."

Laura was hurrying toward us pulling Todd by the hand.

"Wait, Laura," I shouted. "Don't walk so fast. Todd can't take big steps like that."

"What are you talking about? And where have you been? We've been waiting for you for over an hour."

"I'm sorry. I just had the strangest experience. I was in this huge place where everything was enormous. All the door knobs and windows and sinks were way above my head. And there were giant custodians who moved so fast I couldn't keep up with them. In fact, I kept falling because my head seemed too heavy."

"Daddy, you're kidding us," Ginny laughed.

"No, I'm serious. I even planted a bulb there. Look at the dirt on my hands." I held out my fingers for their inspection but the faint streaks of mud on them seemed to be fading. "Harry didn't mind the dirt; he was a nice guy. . . ."

Laura looked at me as if I were hallucinating. "Maybe you got too much sun this afternoon," she said gently. "I think we should go home now."

"But we didn't have our ice cream," Ginny whined.

"Okay, we'll have our treat," I told her, "and then we'll go home. Todd may want to plant some bulbs with me."

I took Todd's little hand in mine and deliberately took small steps that were the same size as his. "I'll ask them for a small spoon for your ice cream, Todd," I told him.

"Daddy, you're different," Ginny observed. "This morning you were mad at Todd."

"I was mad when he spilled his cereal. But I didn't know then what it was like to be small when everyone else was big. I know now, because when I went up those steps I was the smallest person. Everyone else was a giant."

They were looking at me again in disbelief. There was no way they could understand. I couldn't even explain it to myself. I only knew that somehow I had revisited the earliest years — *The World of the Child* that vanishes so mysteriously from the memory of every human being.

About the Author . . . .

As a mother and teacher Aline Wolf has drawn much of her inspiration from the insights of Maria Montessori, and she has highlighted these insights in all her published work.

Mrs. Wolf's books, published by Parent Child Press, include: *A Parents' Guide to the Montessori Classroom* (English and Spanish editions); *Tutoring is Caring — You Can Help Someone to Read*; *Look at the Child* — photographs of young children combined with quotations from Maria Montessori; *A Book About Anna* — a picture book for pre-schoolers with an instructive afterword for parents.

"The World of the Child," Mrs. Wolf says, "was also inspired by Maria Montessori. It is based remotely on an imaginative situation, called *School For Parents*, which Dr. Montessori (1870-1952) used as an illustration in many of her lectures."

Mrs. Wolf and her husband are the parents of nine children and the co-founders of Penn-Mont Academy, the first Montessori school to be licensed in Pennsylvania. A graduate of Marywood College and the St. Nicholas Training Centre for the Montessori Method of Education, she has served on the faculties of the University of Pittsburgh and Pennsylvania State University. Mrs. Wolf has also designed a group of posters which focus on the adult-child relationship.

About the Illustrator . . .

Anna Marie Magagna's career ranges from the illustration of children's books to high fashion illustration and package design. Her book illustrations include the classic, *Five Little Peppers* (MacMillan); *Read Me A Poem* (Grosset & Dunlap); *The Bible for Children* (Standard Education Society of Chicago).

Ms. Magagna's work has been exhibited in one-woman and group shows at the Society of Illustrators in New York City and in the Raymond Burr Gallery on the west coast. Her drawings for Pearl S. Buck's book, *Christmas Miniature*, were shown in the National Gallery of Art, Washington, D.C., and her work is included in the New York Historical Society's "Two Hundred Years of American Illustration."

After graduating from Marywood College in Fine Arts and Drama, Ms. Magagna continued her studies at the Art Students League and the School of Visual Arts in New York City. She has served on the faculty of Pratt Institute in New York City and the Newark School of Fine and Industrial Art in New Jersey. Ms. Magagna resides in New York City where she is an active member of the Society of Illustrators.

Book Design: Robert Cuevas